W9-AHA-948

GEORGE AND MARTHA
ONE MORE TIME

For My Father

The stories in this book were originally published by
Houghton Mifflin Company in *George and Martha: Rise and Shine*, 1976.

Houghton Mifflin Books for Children is an imprint of Houghton Mifflin
Harcourt Publishing Company.

www.hmhbooks.com

Library of Congress Cataloging-in-Publication Data is on file.
ISBN-13: 978-0-547-14423-8

Printed in Singapore

TWP 10 9 8 7 6 5 4 3 2 1

3144

GEORGE AND MARTHA
ONE MORE TIME

written and illustrated by
JAMES MARSHALL

HOUGHTON MIFFLIN BOOKS FOR CHILDREN
HOUGHTON MIFFLIN HARCOURT
BOSTON • NEW YORK • 2009

STORY NUMBER ONE

THE SCARY MOVIE!

Martha was nervous.

"I've never been to a scary movie before."

"Silly goose," said George. "*Everyone* likes scary movies."

"I hope I don't faint," said Martha.

Martha *liked* the scary movie. "This is fun,"
she giggled.

Martha noticed that George was hiding
under his seat.

"I'm looking for my glasses," said George.

"You don't wear glasses," said Martha.

When the movie was over, George was as white as a sheet.

"Hold my hand," George said to Martha.

"I don't want you to be afraid walking home."

"Thank you," said Martha.

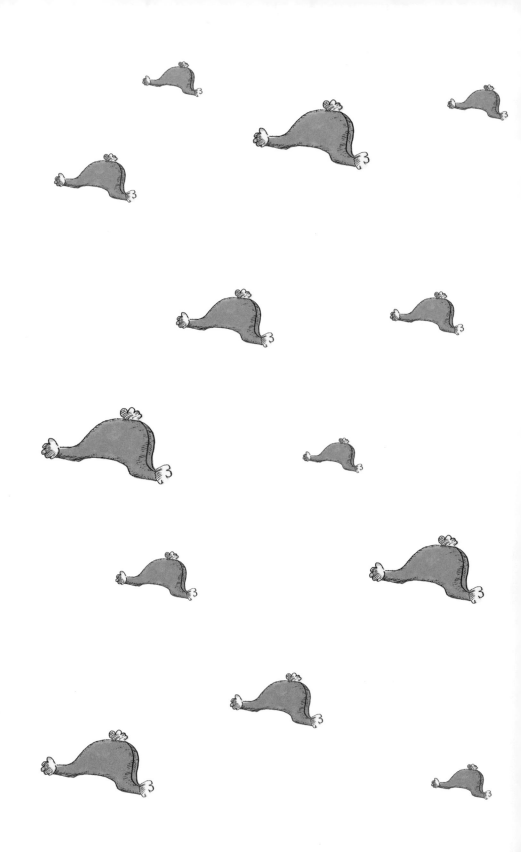

STORY NUMBER Two

THE SECRET CLUB

"Where are you going, George?" asked Martha.

"I'm going to my secret club," said George.

"I'll come along," said Martha.

"Oh no," said George, "it's a secret club."

"But you can let *me* in," said Martha.

"No I can't," said George. And he went on his way.

Martha was furious.

15

When George was inside his secret clubhouse, Martha made a terrible fuss.

"You let me in," she shouted.

"No," said George.

"Yes, yes," cried Martha.

"No, no," said George.

"I'm coming in whether you like it or *not!*"
cried Martha.

When Martha saw the inside of George's clubhouse, she was so ashamed.

"You old sweetheart," she said to George.

George smiled. "I hope you've learned your lesson."

"I certainly have," said his friend.

JAMES MARSHALL (1942–1992)

is one of the most popular and celebrated artists in the field of children's literature. Three of his books were selected as New York Times Best Illustrated Books, and he received a Caldecott Honor Award in 1989 for *Goldilocks and the Three Bears*. With more than seventy-five books to his credit, including the popular George and Martha series, Marshall has earned the admiration and love of countless readers.